SNAKES WEAR SOCKS

CD Hullinger

BY KYLE AND KATY CHANDLER-ISACKSEN
ILLUSTRATED BY CD HULLINGER

Published by
Martin Pearl Publishing
P.O. Box 1441, Dixon, CA 95620

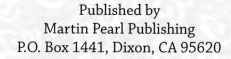

Martin Pearl
PUBLISHING

First Edition: November 2011
ISBN: 9780981482293
Library of Congress Control Number: 2011929903

PRINTED IN THE UNITED STATES OF AMERICA

10 9 8 7 6 5 4 3 2 1

Some mornings are so perfect, so crisp and fresh, that you have to get outside to play as fast as you can. Monday morning was just like that for Jeremy Jones.

Jeremy sprang from bed, slipped on a pair of pants, wiggled into a warm shirt, and looked for his favorite pair of socks—the red ones with the white stars on them. But he could find only one.

"Where's my other sock?" he asked himself, puzzled.

He looked under his bed. He looked behind his dresser. He even looked in his fish bowl. But Jeremy could not find his other sock.

So he put on a different pair of socks, ate his breakfast, and dashed outside to play.

Tuesday was another perfect fall day, just right for crashing and flopping through piles of leaves.

Jeremy pulled on a pair of pants and a fuzzy sweater and looked for his second-most-favorite socks—they were green with white-and-black cows on them. But again he could find only one.

"Where's my other sock?" he asked, even more puzzled than the day before.

He looked under the rug. He looked in his toy chest. He even looked in his piggy bank. But he could not find his missing sock.

So Jeremy put on another pair of socks and ran outside to play.

The rest of the week was just the same.

He couldn't find one of his black socks on Wednesday.

A yellow spaceship sock was missing on Thursday.

And on Friday his super comfy old blue sock with the hole in it was nowhere to be found.

Finally, Jeremy ran to ask his mom if she knew where his socks were.

"Mom, I can't find my socks anywhere! Have you seen them?"

Mom was making applesauce.

"No, Jeremy, I haven't seen them. Did you ask your grandpa?"

Jeremy's grandpa was outside tending to the horses.

"Pop, have you seen my socks?" Jeremy asked.

Grandpa straightened up and smiled. "No, sir. No socks around here."

Jeremy was perplexed. "I'm missing one sock from each of my favorite pairs."

"Did you say you're missing one sock from each pair?" asked Grandpa.

"Yes. And I've looked everywhere."

"Hmmm," Grandpa nodded his head thoughtfully. "I think I know what happened to your socks."

"What, Pop? What?" Jeremy was eager to solve this mystery.

"Snakes have your socks."

"What? Snakes don't wear socks, Pop!" laughed Jeremy. He thought Grandpa was being silly.

"Well, what time of year is it?" asked Grandpa.

"Um, it's autumn."

"And what happens in autumn, Jeremy?"

"Leaves fall off the trees," replied Jeremy

"And what else?"

Jeremy thought for a moment. "It gets colder."

"Exactly!" said Grandpa. "Snakes have your socks."

The next day was Saturday, and Jeremy had a soccer game. He put on his soccer shorts and his soccer shirt.

Then he looked for his soccer socks but could find only one. This time he went straight to his mom.

"Mom, now I can't find one of my soccer socks!" he said, close to tears.

"Oh, Jeremy," Mom said soothingly. "Did you ask your grandfather?"

"I did, and he said snakes have my socks."

"Snakes don't wear socks," Mom smiled.

"I know. That's what I told him!" Jeremy exclaimed.

At the soccer game Jeremy noticed that

all of the other kids were missing socks, too.

As soon as he got home from the game, Jeremy ran straight to his grandpa in the pumpkin patch.

"Pop!" he called excitedly. "All the kids at my soccer game were missing socks!"

Grandpa smiled mysteriously and said, "Is that right?"

He plopped a pumpkin into his wheelbarrow. "Snakes have their socks too, I reckon."

"But Pop, snakes don't wear socks!" Jeremy insisted.

"Jeremy," Pop explained patiently. "It will soon be winter, and the days are getting colder. Snakes need to stay warm, so they're snuggled into your socks in their winter den. Now, if you want to find your socks, where's a warm place to look for them?"

Jeremy thought...and thought... and thought some more.

He had it!

"I would go to the heater room in the basement!"

So Jeremy ran into the house, raced through the living room, and sprinted down the basement stairs.

He opened
the door to
the heater room
and reached for the light.
CLICK!

He found his socks.
He found everybody's socks!

Jeremy stared.
The snakes stared back.
Jeremy blinked.
The snakes flicked their tongues.

Finally, a garter snake in his comfy old blue sock with the hole in it asked,

"Would you mind closing that door? You are letting in the cold!"

"Oh. Sure," Jeremy said. He
closed the door and slowly
climbed the stairs.

"Did you ever find your socks, honey?" his mom asked as she walked into the living room.

Jeremy giggled at Pop. Pop winked at Jeremy.

"Yep! Snakes have my socks."

And with that he ran outside to play.

Jeremy had solved the mystery of the missing socks and was happy the snakes would be warm through the winter.

As for getting his socks back...

...He could wait until spring.

Snake Facts

Snakes don't really wear socks when it gets cold. So how do they stay warm during winter?

First of all, snakes are reptiles. And reptiles are cold-blooded. Cold-blooded means their bodies are the same temperature as their surroundings.

Warm-blooded animals like mammals and birds, are very different. Warm-blooded animals have an internal "furnace" that keeps them warm in all kinds of weather. They aren't dependent on the temperature around them to keep warm.

If the world around a snake is warm, the way it is in the summer, the snake is warm. And when snakes are warm, they are very active. They slither about, hunt for food, grow, and even shed their skins once they outgrow them.

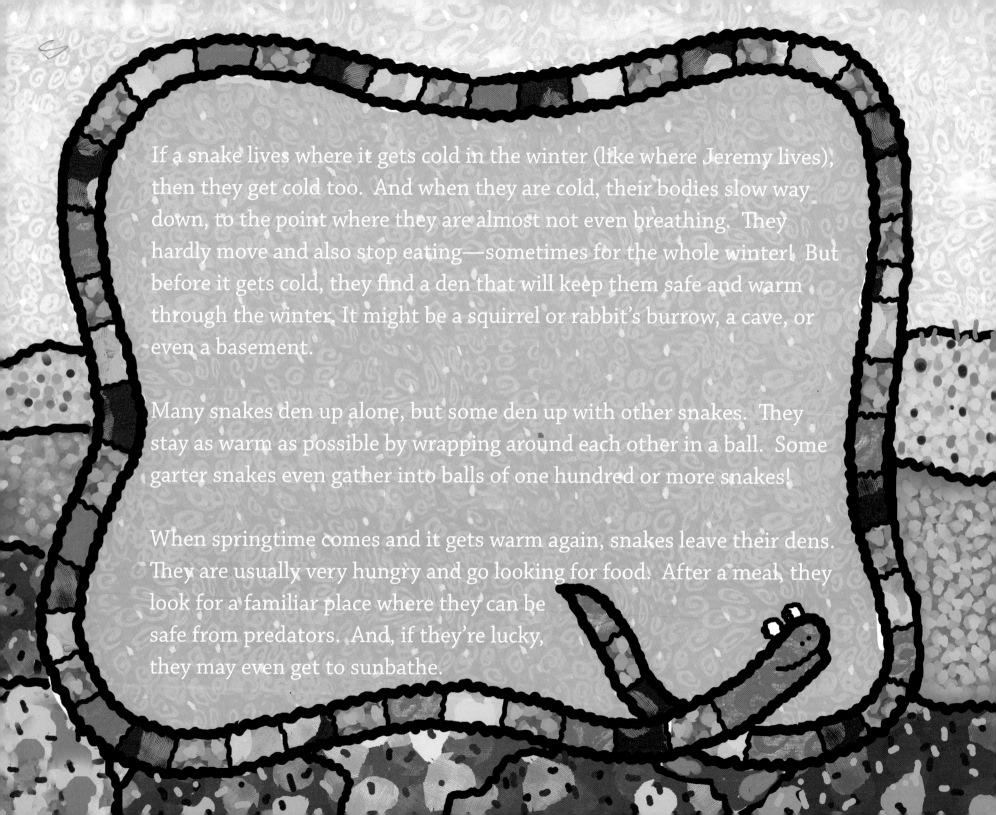

If a snake lives where it gets cold in the winter (like where Jeremy lives), then they get cold too. And when they are cold, their bodies slow way down, to the point where they are almost not even breathing. They hardly move and also stop eating—sometimes for the whole winter! But before it gets cold, they find a den that will keep them safe and warm through the winter. It might be a squirrel or rabbit's burrow, a cave, or even a basement.

Many snakes den up alone, but some den up with other snakes. They stay as warm as possible by wrapping around each other in a ball. Some garter snakes even gather into balls of one hundred or more snakes!

When springtime comes and it gets warm again, snakes leave their dens. They are usually very hungry and go looking for food. After a meal, they look for a familiar place where they can be safe from predators. And, if they're lucky, they may even get to sunbathe.